1

The Bytes Brothers
INPUT AN INVESTIGATION

This Armada book belongs to:

_____

_____

_____

The Bytes Brothers
INPUT AN INVESTIGATION

A Solve-it-Yourself Computer Mystery

THE BYTES BROTHERS INPUT AN INVESTIGATION is a collection of five mystery stories, each of which includes a computer program that helps schoolboys Brent and Barry Bytes to solve the mystery. Readers can type the programs into their own home or school computer and thus recreate the Bytes Brothers' solutions for themselves.

The programs, written in Bytes Brothers BASIC, have been designed to work on all micro-computers and have been tested on the leading home computers on the market.

The programs are accompanied by an extensive 'de-bugging' section which explains how they work, and, where necessary, how they can be adapted for different computers.

About the authors

Lois and Floyd McCoy are a husband-and-wife team who together create the Bytes Brothers mysteries and write the programs. Lois McCoy, a journalist with a scientific background, and Floyd McCoy, an oceanographer at Columbia University and a volcanologist, have four children. They live in New York State, in a converted barn, and spend their summers in the scientific village of Woods Hole, Cape Cod.

The Bytes Brothers

INPUT AN INVESTIGATION

A Solve-it-Yourself
Computer Mystery

LOIS & FLOYD McCOY

Illustrations by Leslie Morrill

An Armada Original

THE BYTES BROTHERS INPUT AN INVESTIGATION
was first published in the U.K. in 1983
in Armada by Fontana Paperbacks,
8 Grafton Street, London W1X 3LA

Reproduced, printed and bound in Great Britain by
Hazell Watson & Viney Limited,
Member of the BPCC Group,
Aylesbury, Bucks

```
1000 PRINT "DEDICATED WITH LOVE TO"
1010 PRINT "JILL ELAINE McCOY"
1020 END
```

The authors wish to thank Errol Weiss, Adam Ratner, Douglas Shearer, Dr John La Brecque and Chip Kennedy (Lamont-Doherty Geological Observatory), Timothy Takahashi, Thomas Sullivan (Rockland County [N.Y.] Bureau of Criminal Investigation), David Kopperman, David Fradkin, Edward Moskowitz and Stuart Lewis for technical assistance.

Armada is grateful to Carolyn Hughes and Alex Gollner for their help in checking the British edition.

Contents

LAMONT LANDING —
The Bytes Brothers Home Town

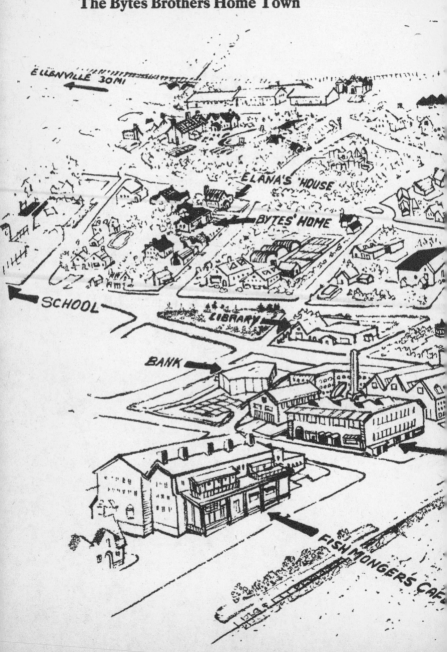

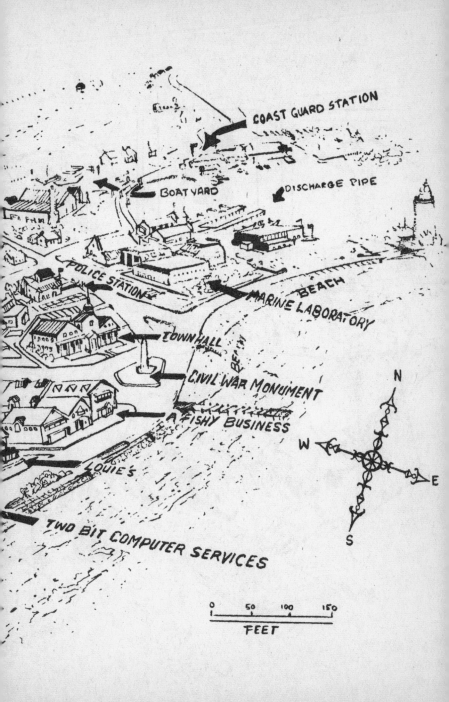

COAST GUARD STATION

BOAT YARD

DISCHARGE PIPE

POLICE STATION

MARINE BEACH LABORATORY

BEACH

TOWN HALL

CIVIL WAR MONUMENT

A FISHY BUSINESS

LOUIE'S

TWO BIT COMPUTER SERVICES

N
W   E
S

0   50   100   150
FEET

1.

Footsteps in the Snow

Brent Bytes was in bed when his older brother Barry got home from school. Brent had a bad case of the chicken pox and was asleep.

Thirteen-year-old Barry collapsed on to his own bed and began a new mystery book, glancing at his eleven-year-old brother between murders.

After a while Brent stretched. "I feel so horrible that I can't even enjoy missing school," he moaned.

Barry felt sorry for him. He knew there was only one thing that might make Brent forget his throbbing head and spotted body: Nibble.

Nibble was the Bytes brothers' nickname for their home computer, which sat on the long table between their beds.

Barry put his book down and pressed Nibble's ON switch. "Holy macro," he said as his fingers played musical microcircuits on the keyboard. "Why can't Nibble do what we want him to do, instead of what we tell him to do?"

Brent, his eyes still closed, just barely smiled. His expression suggested that a full grin would be torture.

"Don't get angry at Nibble, Barry." His usually loud voice was faint. "It's just being logical, as always." His eyelids, each weighing a ton, did a one-second butterfly imitation before slamming shut again.

Barry gave up. Brent, who usually seemed to have jumping beans in his socks, must really be sick. Barry picked up his book and went downstairs to the kitchen.

He was sitting at the kitchen table with a slice of chocolate cake, a glass of milk, and his open book in front of him as his mother came in the back door. Dr Bytes was a marine biologist; she worked in a laboratory that was about a ten-minute walk from the Bytes' home.

When Barry told her Brent was upstairs snoozing, she thought about her rambunctious younger son as she began to cut onions and potatoes for a pot of stew. "If he's asleep, he's *sick*. I'm going to send Dad an electronic mail message as soon as I'm done slicing these vegetables." Mr Bytes owned a business, Two-Bit Computer Services, and was out of town that day, taking care of some business at Dutchtown Computer Wholesalers. "He'll probably want to drive home tonight to be with Brent if he can arrange it."

Brent hardly blinked an eye as his mother and brother came quietly into his bedroom a few minutes later. Dr Bytes then picked up the phone and dialled the electronic mail's telephone number. When she heard a high-pitched data tone, she placed the phone receiver in the cradle-like modem and typed her password.

Then, she typed her message.

```
TO:      DCDST
FROM:    BYTES
SUBJECT:MESSAGE FOR MARK BYTES
```

1) Brent has the chicken pox, and feels
    like a strand of spaghetti. He looks
    as if he were splattered with
    spaghetti sauce. Perhaps, you'd like
    to come home earlier than you had
    planned.

Jill

Bye

```
Send?    YES
Msg posted  Dec 10   3:50 PM  EST
Msg          31BYTES-1937-6592
This mail session is now complete.
```

Nibble, in direct connection with a computer hundreds of miles away, transmitted the message.

A while later Dr Bytes asked Nibble to check if there was an answer in the Bytes "mailbox". There was.

```
Msg posted  Dec 10   4:00 PM  EST
Msg          97CDST-1941-6594
```

```
To:      BYTES
From:    DCDST
Subject:BRENT'S CHICKEN POX
```

1) I shall arrive home tonight,
   after 1:00 AM.

Mark

Bye

When Brent awoke in the morning, he was feeling a bit better. He glanced out of the window opposite his bed. The bare maple tree limbs had a white coating of snow. "Darn," said Brent sourly to himself. "The first snow of the year and I'm stuck in bed."

Downstairs, Dr Bytes and her husband were sitting at the kitchen table drinking their coffee. Barry walked into the kitchen as the telephone rang, and picked up the receiver.

"It's Jimmy," Barry said to his parents. "He wants to know if he can borrow Brent's sledge since Brent won't be able to use it. Should I go and ask Brent if it's OK?"

"Brent's not up yet," said Mr Bytes as he glanced at the kitchen clock. It was just nine o'clock. "But I'm sure he won't mind. Jimmy's one of his best friends."

"Brent's going to be miserable when he sees that there's been a snowfall," said Dr Bytes.

Barry was anxious to go outside and play in the snow himself. "Look! The snow just stopped," he said excitedly. "Brother, is it deep. It must have started right when I went to sleep."

Mr Bytes shook his head. "When I drove into the driveway at about one o'clock this morning, the first snowflakes were just beginning to fall."

Barry was finishing his breakfast when there was a knock on the door. Mr Bytes was surprised to see Jimmy standing there with a hang-dog look on his face. "Good morning, Jim. You can go right into the garage and get the sledge."

"Oh, Mr Bytes, you don't understand." Jimmy sounded terribly upset. "I've already been to the garage and the sledge isn't there. Someone must have stolen it!"

"That's odd," said Mr Bytes. "It was there last night when I got home. The falling snowflakes made me think of it. I'm sure it was there, in the corner where we always keep it."

"Come in anyway, Jimmy, and warm up," said Dr Bytes.

Later, after Jimmy had let himself out of the front door, Mr Bytes thought about the missing sledge. It was in the garage at one o'clock in the morning. That meant that someone removed it some time after that.

Barry said, "I bet Jimmy took it. He could have gone to the garage and carried it home. Then he could have come back here to knock on our back door."

"No, that's impossible, Barry," said Mr Bytes. "Because when I answered the door and Jimmy told me he already had been to the garage, I looked outside. Let me show you what I saw." Mr Bytes picked up a pencil and started sketching on the edge of the morning newspaper. This is what he drew: *(See over)*

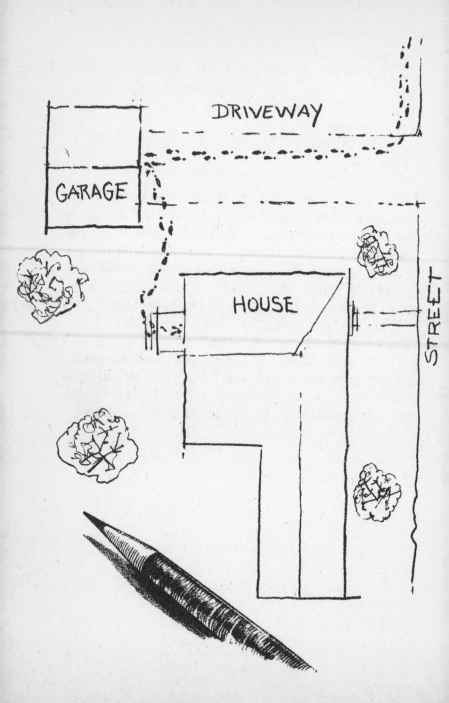

"Mom!" Just then Brent called from the upstairs bedroom. "Could I have a cup of tea?"

A few minutes later, Barry, carrying a mug of tea sweetened with honey, walked into the bedroom and told Brent the bad news.

"But I can't believe that Jim would take my sledge," Brent muttered.

"Don't you remember how Jim loved that sledge?" Barry spoke softly but had a very determined look on his face. "Remember the time he tried to buy it from you?"

Brent leaned forward and took a small sip of his tea, dribbling a few drops on his pyjamas. "Yes, but I told him that I'd never sell it because it had been my grandfather's and they don't even make sledges like that any more."

"I know Jim's your friend," said Barry, "and that you think he wouldn't take anything from you. But there's something suspicious about the sledge disappearing, and I think Jim has something to do with it."

Dr Bytes stood in the bedroom door. "Barry, maybe you're over-reacting. After all, Jim called to ask permission to borrow the sledge. I can't imagine he'd do that if he had stolen it." She shook her head, thinking. "But how could anyone have stolen it? There were no footprints from the garage."

"Good morning, my polka-dotted son. How do you feel?" Brent gave his father a "so-so" look as Mr Bytes walked into the room and turned to his wife. "You know, Jill, you're right. It's weird. Jim's prints go to the garage, not away from it."

Brent sighed. "It makes me *sicker* to think that a friend of mine stole my sledge . . . ."

Barry turned to his younger brother. "Brent, don't worry about it. I'll solve the mystery. You lie back and rest and let me take care of it."

For once, Brent didn't have much energy, so he decided to let his brother try to solve the mystery alone. One thing was for sure. There was no way that Jim stole that sledge after one a.m. His bedtime was nine p.m.! And Brent knew Jimmy well enough to know that he couldn't sneak out of his house in the middle of the night.

An hour later, Brent looked out of his window at the snow in the backyard. He could see Jimmy's footprints leading from the street to the garage and then to the back porch. Leaning over one of the prints was Barry, a tape measure in his hand. Brent knew his big brother was on to something.

Soon Barry came into the kitchen, stamping the snow from his boots as he hung up his down-filled parka. Then he went upstairs.

"How are you doing?" asked Brent anxiously, as Barry sat down in front of Nibble and began to type.

"Shhh. I can't concentrate when you're talking to me."

Barry typed, then stopped to study the readout. Then he typed again for a few minutes. As he read, his forehead began to resemble a prune because he was concentrating so hard.

Suddenly Barry stopped. He took a long hard look at Nibble's monitor. This was what he saw:

```
1000 REM FOOTSTEPS PROGRAM
1010 PRINT "ENTER FOOTSTEP DEPTH"
1020 PRINT "BETWEEN STREET AND"
1030 PRINT "GARAGE"
1040 INPUT A
1050 PRINT "ENTER FOOTSTEP DEPTH"
1060 PRINT "BETWEEN GARAGE AND"
1070 PRINT "HOUSE"
1080 INPUT B
1090 LET C=A/B
1100 PRINT "FOOTSTEPS BETWEEN STREET"
1110 PRINT "AND GARAGE ARE ";C;" TIMES"
1120 PRINT "AS DEEP AS THOSE BETWEEN"
1130 PRINT "GARAGE AND HOUSE"
1140 END
```

Next Barry debugged the program. (Checking to be sure a program makes sense, then searching for errors and correcting them is called *debugging*):

1000 REM FOOTSTEPS PROGRAM
Computer programs need a number [like 1000] at the beginning of each line. Lines are usually numbered by tens, in case you need to add one or more lines in between.

REM is short for *REMARK*. When Barry typed REM at the beginning of the line, this told Nibble to ignore the statement. Barry only put it there to help himself.

1010 PRINT "ENTER FOOTSTEP DEPTH"
1020 PRINT "BETWEEN STREET AND"
1030 PRINT "GARAGE"
1040 INPUT A

The word PRINT told Nibble to ask this as a question in the actual program-run [on page 25]. All PRINT statements must be within quotation marks. Barry measured the street-to-garage prints. [They were 9 inches deep.] He decided to use the symbol A to stand for these prints. INPUT tells the computer to stop and wait for data. In the program-run, at Line 1040, Nibble will ask Barry to INPUT his footprint information then.

1050 PRINT "ENTER FOOTSTEP DEPTH"
1060 PRINT "BETWEEN GARAGE AND"
1070 PRINT "HOUSE"
1080 INPUT B

These measured 3 inches. Barry had B stand for them. Nibble's memory automatically stores all information Barry types in after the word INPUT.

1090 LET C=A/B

Barry set up his equation; C would be the answer. Writing LET C =means that C takes the value of whatever is to the right of the equal sign. So C has the same value as A divided by B. The footprints between the street and the garage are C times as deep as those leading from the garage to the house. So . . . A = C times B which is the same as C = A divided by B. A slash [/] means divide the first number by the second.

1100 PRINT "FOOTSTEPS BETWEEN STREET"
1110 PRINT "AND GARAGE ARE ";C;" TIMES"
1120 PRINT "AS DEEP AS THOSE BETWEEN"
1130 PRINT "GARAGE AND HOUSE"

Here is how Nibble was instructed to give Barry the answer. Notice how the semicolons [around C] are placed. They separate the different parts of a PRINT statement. Notice that C is not within the quotation marks because the value of C will be supplied by Nibble.

NOTE: For computers with less than 24-character displays, split lines 1100-1130 into five lines.

1140 END

Tells Nibble the program is finished. This line could be left out.

Everything looked good, so he ran the program:

```
ENTER FOOTSTEP DEPTH
BETWEEN STREET AND
GARAGE
?9
```

Nibble automatically asked this question.
Barry typed in the answer, after the ?.

```
ENTER FOOTSTEP DEPTH
BETWEEN GARAGE AND
HOUSE
?3
```

The answer was input by Barry.

```
FOOTSTEPS BETWEEN STREET
AND GARAGE ARE 3 TIMES
AS DEEP AS THOSE BETWEEN
GARAGE AND HOUSE
```

Nibble output the answer.

Barry sighed deeply. He leaned back in his chair, turning towards Brent.

Brent knew his brother very well. He knew a solution had been found when Barry got that certain satisfied Cheshire Cat look.

But this time Brent wasn't sure if he wanted to know the solution. He was worried that Jim might be involved. He's my friend, Brent thought to himself. I don't want to find out that he did something he shouldn't have.

"Well?" Brent asked reluctantly. "Was it Jimmy?"

"Yes, Brent. I'm sorry to have to tell you. But I know how Jimmy stole the sledge. And I know how he managed to leave no footprints, too."

DO YOU KNOW
how Barry solved the crime?

The computer analysis of the footprints told Barry that, although the same-size boot made all the prints, either a heavier person or someone carrying a load made the prints from the street to the garage. These prints were deeper. Barry then realized that Jimmy must have come to the garage earlier in the morning, stolen the sledge, and walked backwards in his footprints, carrying the sledge. After hiding the sledge in his own garage loft, Jim called Brent's house, asking to borrow the sledge.

When confronted with the evidence, Jimmy admitted stealing the sledge, then calling to borrow it so he wouldn't be suspected.

Jim returned the sledge, apologized sheepishly, and shovelled snow for the Bytes family for three hours.

2.

A Marble-filled Jar

Twelve-year-old Elana Lynsky and her mother lived next door to the Bytes family.

Elana had a talent for getting Brent's goat. She enjoyed poking fun at his love for computer science. "Hey, hacker, why aren't you playing with Dribble?"

"Nibble," corrected Brent crossly. He hated when Elana called him a hacker—that meant he was computer-crazy. It made him so mad that he never even noticed how she was always manoeuvering situations so *she* could be near Nibble.

Elana was a secret hacker!

"Let's go up to your room," said Elana. "If you insist upon staring at Dribble's monitor hour after hour, I'll force myself to keep you company, even though you know I can't stand it."

Brent grinned. He liked his neighbour, even when she was teasing him. "I can't. I have to go to Louie's to buy some milk. Want to come?"

Louie's Grocery Store was three blocks away. Brent and Elana entered the store and were heading for the refrigeration unit in the back when Brent bumped into a rack with small plastic toys and balloons.

"Look, Elana." He pointed towards a marble-filled jar next to the balloons with a sign below it.

GUESS
THE CORRECT NUMBER
of
MARBLES
IN THE JAR
AND WIN
$5!
WINNER
TO BE ANNOUNCED
NEXT TUESDAY

Elana turned to Brent, "What'll we do? Try to count 'em?"

Brent shook his head. "Come on. I've got an idea." He started for home.

Dr Bytes, Brent's mother, was sitting at her desk checking her laboratory notes. "Just put the milk in the 'fridge, Brent," she said without raising her head.

"Oh oh. . ." whispered Elana as she followed Brent's climb up the stairs, two at a time.

"We'll be going back to the store soon, and we can get the milk then," Brent said distractedly as he searched through his cupboard.

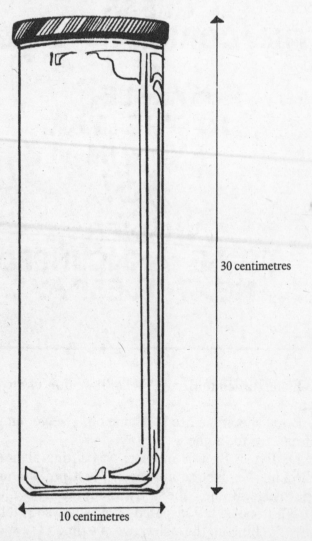

30 centimetres

10 centimetres

"Ah hah!" In his hands was a jar exactly like the marble-filled one at Louie's.

"But," said Elana, "where will we get such a huge bunch of marbles?"

Brent smiled and patted his computer. "With Nibble, we don't need marbles." And he explained his plan.

Then they got to work. Together Elana and Brent measured the height and diameter of the jar.

"Now we have to know the diameter of a marble," said Brent as he fished one out of the bottom of a box labelled MISCELLANEOUS.

"We need calipers," said Elana. "I think I saw a pair in your workroom. Come on."

"Right," said Brent, who had no idea what calipers were but wasn't about to let Elana know that.

In the cellar workroom Elana did the measuring. Brent wrote in his notebook:

one marble = 1.5 centimetres in diameter

"I'm really excited," said Elana when they were back in Brent's room, in front of Nibble. Elana opened Barry's geometry textbook as Brent flipped the computer's switch and began to devise a program:

```
1000 REM THIS PROGRAM COMPUTES HOW MANY
1010 REM MARBLES CAN FIT INSIDE A JAR.
1020 PRINT "ENTER THE DIAMETER OF JAR"
1030 INPUT D
1040 PRINT "ENTER THE HEIGHT OF JAR"
1050 INPUT H
1060 PRINT "ENTER THE DIAMETER OF THE M
ARBLE"
1070 INPUT M
1080 REM COMPUTE THE AREA OF THE
1090 REM JAR'S BOTTOM.
1100 LET A=3.14159*(D/2)^2
1110 REM COMPUTE VOLUME OF THE JAR
1120 LET V=A*H
1130 PRINT "ENTER THE PACKING FRACTION"
```

"Packing fraction! What's that?" wondered Elana.

"You don't think," answered Brent, as he studied the program, "that the marbles fill up all of the room inside the jar, do you? There's a theory that states that the most space spherical objects—like marbles—can fill is 74%. We can't forget those empty spaces between the marbles."

Elana looked impressed. "I never thought of that," she said as Brent started typing again.

```
1140 INPUT P
1150 REM COMPUTE THE VOLUME THAT
1160 REM THE PACKED MARBLES OCCUPY.
1170 LET S=V*P
1180 REM COMPUTE THE VOLUME OF ONE MARB
LE.
1190 LET J=(4/3)*3.14159*(M/2)^3
1200 REM FIND NUMBER OF MARBLES IN THE
JAR.
1210 LET N=S/J
1220 LET N=INT(N)
1230 PRINT "THERE ARE ";N;" MARBLES IN
THE JAR."
```

"I wonder if it's OK," said Brent, peering at the monitor.

"Let's go over each step to debug it," said Elana.

1000 REM THIS PROGRAM COMPUTES HOW MANY
1010 REM MARBLES CAN FIT INSIDE A JAR.
These beginning REM [for "remarks"] statements were to help Brent remember what he was doing. As long as he types REM first, the computer will ignore these comments; they're to help humans.

1020 PRINT "ENTER THE DIAMETER OF JAR"
1030 INPUT D
Elana and Brent knew the diameter was 10 centimetres. In this program, D would stand for the jar *diameter*.

1040 PRINT "ENTER THE HEIGHT OF
   JAR"
1050 INPUT H

The *height* of the jar was 30 centimetres.
H was chosen to stand for *height*.

1060 PRINT "ENTER DIAMETER OF
THE MARBLE"
1070 INPUT M

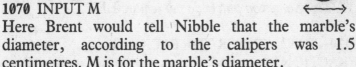

Here Brent would tell Nibble that the marble's
diameter, according to the calipers was 1.5
centimetres. M is for the marble's diameter.

1080 REM COMPUTE THE AREA OF THE
1090 REM JAR'S BOTTOM.
1100 LET A =3.14159*(D/2)∧2

To find out the *area* of any circle, you multiply
3.14159 [which is pi, or π] by the radius [which is ½
of the diameter], squared. Area = πr^2, or, written so
Nibble can understand:

Area = 3.14159 × $\left(\dfrac{\text{diameter}}{2}\right)$2

An asterisk (∗) means *times* or *multiply* in computer
language, and ∧ 2 = squared, and ∧ 3 = cubed.

See line 1190 for another example of this. [Some
computers prefer ↑ instead of ∧. Others use ∗∗.]

1110 REM COMPUTE VOLUME OF THE JAR.
1120 LET V = A*H

To find out the *volume* [or amount of space] in the jar, Brent multiplied the *area* [see lines 1080, 1090, 1100] by the jar's height [see lines 1040, 1050].

Or: Area × Height = Volume.

In computer language you must reverse it and write: LET V = A * H.

NOTE: Some computers do not require LET.

1130 PRINT "ENTER THE PACKING FRACTION"
1140 INPUT P

If you pack spherical objects—like marbles—as tightly together as possible, there will still be space in between:

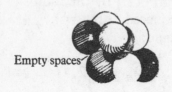

Empty spaces

There is a theory called Packing Fraction that says that the most space the marbles can occupy is 74%, or .74. This means that 26% of the space in the marble-filled jar will be empty [100% minus 74% = 26%]. This is why Elana and Brent typed P [for *packing fraction*] equalling .74. Notice the use of quotation marks in all PRINT statements.

1150 REM COMPUTE THE VOLUME THAT
1160 REM THE PACKED MARBLES OCCUPY.
1170 LET S = V∗P

Once Brent knew the *volume* [or the amount of space within the jar], he could multiply it by the packing fraction [see lines 1130, 1140]. That answer would tell him how much space [S] is available to pack marbles in.

Or: Volume × Packing Fraction = Space in the Jar for Marbles. For Nibble to understand, it must be written as it is in line 1170.

1180 REM COMPUTE VOLUME OF ONE MARBLE
1190 LET J = (4/3)∗3.14159∗(M/2) ↑ 3

The space a marble occupies is its *volume*. Elana discovered the equation for a marble's volume by using the formula from Barry's geometry book:

$V = \frac{4}{3} \pi r^3$ or Marble's Volume = $\frac{4}{3}$ × π × radius^3.
Another way to say the same thing is: Marble's Volume
$= \frac{4}{3} \times 3.14159 \times \left(\dfrac{\text{marble diameter}}{2}\right)3$

See line 1190 for the same equation in computer language.

[Remember: $\wedge$ 3 means you should cube the number — you multiply it times itself three times.]

1200 REM FIND NUMBER OF MARBLES IN JAR.
1210 LET N = S/J

Here's what all this means:
N = number of marbles
S = space for marbles in the jar
J = volume of a marble

If Nibble would divide the available space in the jar by the space one marble occupied, Brent and Elana would know how many marbles could fit in the jar.
Or: N = S ÷ J.

1220 LET N = INT(N)
LET N = INT(N) tells Nibble to 'truncate' N, or change it to a whole number, by omitting the digits after the decimal point.

1230 PRINT "THERE ARE "; N; " MARBLES IN THE JAR."
Notice the use of quotation marks and semicolons, required for Nibble to know what to do.
NOTE: On computers which cannot work out squares and cubes, line 1100 will be:
1100 LET A = 3.14159 * (D /2) * (D /2)
Line 1190 will be:
1190 LET J = (4/3) * 3.14159 * (M/2) * (M/2) * (H/2)

"OK, hacker. You've got it," said Elana, patting Brent on the back as he stood up and stretched. "It all makes sense to me. Let's run it." She sat down and started to punch in their measurements of the jar and the marble.

```
ENTER THE DIAMETER OF JAR
?10
```

Nibble requested this information.
Elana typed ten.

The height was asked for.

```
ENTER THE HEIGHT OF JAR
?30
```

Elana input 30.

```
ENTER THE DIAMETER OF THE MARBLE
?1.5
```

Elana knew the size from the caliper measurement.

```
ENTER THE PACKING FRACTION
?.74
```

Elana typed the packing fraction.

```
THERE ARE 986 MARBLES IN THE JAR.
```

Nibble then output the answer, after truncating it. [Before truncation, it was 986.667.]

Elana turned to Brent. "Well, hacker, you've managed to solve another problem on your dear Dribble," said the secret hacker.

Brent didn't waste time correcting Elana. He raced out of his room and was on the way to Louie's, with Elana close behind.

In the grocery store, a group of kids were surrounding the marble jar like ants on a piece of candy. Everyone was trying to count out loud so they wouldn't lose their place, and they kept mixing each other up. Tempers were wearing thin. Except for Kevin Klupp's.

Kevin, Louie's nephew, was watching all the kids with a satisfied smile on his face.

"Louie," said Brent breathlessly as he stumbled over a carton of soap. "I know how many marbles are in your jar."

"Don't forget the milk," said Elana as she jogged up to them.

Elana and Brent stood for a few minutes in front of the rack of balloons, staring at the jar filled with marbles. They discussed how they would spend the five dollars. Elana was going to put her $2.50 in her bank account. (She was secretly saving to buy her very own Dribble.) Brent planned to buy a Louisville Slugger baseball bat. Kevin Klupp stood and listened to them, as he played with a bag of balloons.

A week later, Brent knocked on Elana's door. "Come on. Let's go to Louie's. It's time for him to announce the winners — us!"

"The correct answer," said Louie before a group of seven kids, "is 520. And the winner is my nephew, Kevin Klupp."

"Louie, there's got to be some mistake," said Elana, completely bewildered. "I *know* that a jar of that size, measuring 30 centimetres by 10 centimetres, filled with marbles measuring 1.5 centimetres in diameter, will hold 986 marbles."

"I'm sorry, Elana. I know you and Brent worked hard to calculate the answer. But I'm afraid that Kevin's guess is closest." Louie really did look sorry.

"That's right," said John, the stock boy. "This morning I spent an hour in the back room counting the marbles. Kevin came closest."

"How could that be?" pondered Brent as he walked home, with Elana at his side.

"I don't understand," said Elana dejectedly. "It must be Dribble's fault."

"Elana, Nibble is a tool." Brent looked serious. "It can only do what we tell it to do. It does make us give it sensible step-by-step information, though. I know we measured the jar correctly. I know we measured the marble correctly. If we gave that information to Nibble, there is no way that we would be given the wrong answer." Elana walked towards her front porch, shaking her head as Brent added, "Nibble is very user-friendly . . . . I just can't figure out what happened."

Brent was on his bed, absentmindedly turning the pages of one of Barry's mystery books, when his father walked in. "Hi, Brent. Did you get your share of the five dollars?"

Brent told his father what had happened. Mr Bytes sat down on the edge of Barry's bed and looked at the printout of the program that Brent and Elana had run.

"There's nothing wrong with this. If the jar is the size you told your computer it is, and if you measured the marble correctly, you have the right answer."

In his mind Brent pictured the jar at Louie's. He knew exactly what it looked like because he'd stopped in to stare at it several times during the past week. There it was, right next to the wire stand with the packages of balloons.

"Wait a minute!" Brent flew off his bed, ran outside, and yelled at Elana who was staring out into space from the safety of her front porch. He headed for Louie's. Elana was smart enough to jump off the porch and follow at top speed, without asking questions.

"Louie," said Brent as he spotted the owner, "I've figured out what happened and I don't think it was fair."

DO YOU KNOW
what Brent realised?

Upon questioning Louie, Brent found out that it was Kevin Klupp himself who filled the jar with the marbles. Louie had been busy waiting on customers and didn't actually *see* his nephew fill the jar. But Louie was sure that Kevin hadn't counted them because he heard his nephew pour the bag of marbles all at once into the jar.

What Louie didn't know was that, before pouring in the marbles, Kevin took a package of balloons from the rack, blew up a long white one, and inserted it directly in the centre of the jar.

When John the stock boy counted the marbles, he assumed that Louie himself had placed the balloon inside. He didn't think it was right to try and trick the children, but Louie was his employer so John kept the information to himself.

When Louie was told what his nephew Kevin had done, he refilled the jar with marbles without the balloon, and made Kevin count them. Brent and Elana were then awarded the prize money.

Louie ordered Kevin to help John in the back room after school for the rest of the month.

3

The Science Project

Barry dropped his books on the desk as Pearl Larkin entered the classroom. "Hi, Pearl," said Barry as she passed his desk.

"Hello, Barry." Pearl wore a wide smile. She walked straight over to the teacher. "Ms Seal, I brought in my science project for the competition. Wait till you see it!" In Pearl's hand was a tiny paper bag.

"Well, it certainly won't take up much space, Pearl!" said Ms Seal, as she looked in the bag. Inside was a plastic model of a human cell. "Why, it's beautiful. How creative of you!" She handed the bag back to Pearl. "I thought we'd keep the projects in that old cabinet in the back room until the judging. Do you know the one I mean? With the glass shelves?"

Pearl nodded. She headed for the small hallway area, referred to as the back room. Along with the cabinet, Ms Seal kept supplies on the table, and there was a deep sink for rinsing frog-dissecting instruments.

"Oh, Pearl," called Ms Seal. "I meant to clean that cabinet. It hasn't been used for years and it's quite dusty. Would you mind wiping it with a paper towel and some water?"

As Pearl worked on the cabinet shelves, students milled about the classroom, working on their projects.

Except for Belinda, who sat in the last desk closest to the back room. She took a bottle of clear nail polish from her pocket. She obviously wasn't working on her science project.

As Pearl wiped the glass shelves, one slipped off its support. It wouldn't go back on.

"Belinda?" Pearl peered around the corner. "Could you help me for a minute with this shelf?"

"Sorry, Pearl, I can't. I just put on nail polish." Belinda sat with her palms up, waiting for the polish to dry.

"Never mind, I fixed it," said Pearl.

"What did you make for the science competition?" asked Belinda.

"Promise you won't tell anyone? I bet it wins." The student with the best science project would spend a day in a research laboratory, working side-by-side with a scientist.

Belinda, her palms still up, peered into the bag that Pearl held open for her.

"Wow," she said. "What a cell."

Barry, who sat next to Belinda, was just walking back to his desk. "Can I see, Pearl?" June, who sat in front of Barry, resembled a turtle as she strained her neck to look too.

Just then Ms Seal asked everyone to sit down. "I'll show you after class," Pearl whispered to Barry. She quickly placed the little bag on the top shelf in the cabinet and headed for her own desk.

After class, Barry called to Pearl as she headed out of the room. "You were going to show me your project, remember?"

Pearl smiled. She loved showing it off. And Barry

was a friend. He wouldn't steal her idea, or tell anyone else about it. She and Barry walked to the back room and Pearl opened the cabinet.

The little paper bag was gone.

"Someone took my cell!" exclaimed Pearl. "And whoever did it knew it was good because Ms Seal said so. Some kid stole it so I wouldn't win."

"But who would do that?" asked Barry. Barry sat right near the back of the classroom and could see anyone who went back there. Only a couple of people had been in the back room today.

"If you can remember everyone who walked back there, maybe we could figure out who took it." Pearl looked determined.

"Let's see." Barry put his thinking cap on. "June went back there to wash her hands."

"Supposedly. I bet she stole my project."

"Well," said Barry, "she *did* have paint all over her hands."

"A decoy." Pearl was taking the loss badly.

"Then there was Belinda. She washed her hands too, I guess."

"Oh. Belinda took it, I bet. She could have slipped it into her pocket. She wore pants today. A perfect way to steal it."

"Aw, come on," said Barry. Every boy in the class had pants pockets, and so did most of the girls. "Be reasonable."

"Who else?"

"Neil Travis. I think he got some graph paper."

"Neil. He doesn't like me. I bet he did it."

Barry ignored this. "I think that's it. Belinda, June, Neil."

"Oh, Barry. How am I going to get my project back? I worked so hard on it. It was so perfect."

"Listen, Pearl, calm down. If there's a way to solve this mystery, I'll think of it. Now let's look at the situation logically."

Pearl wrung her hands. "I'm thinking logically. We have three suspects. How do we figure out which one is a criminal? When I find him, I'll have him jailed and I'll throw away the key."

Good grief, Barry thought to himself. Out loud, he said, "I know how the police would handle this. They'd search for fingerprints."

Pearl and Barry looked at one another, got up at the same time, and headed for the cabinet. On the top shelf, where Pearl had placed her paper bag, there were marks—smudges really.

"Great," said Barry. "Give me your pencil."

Holding the pencil over the top shelf, Barry scratched the point with a paper clip. Black powder started to collect on the shelf. Pearl was wearing a small gold pin on her blouse, a little goose with a real tail feather. She unpinned it and with the feather she gently dusted the black graphite all over the smudges.

An arch and whorl pattern of two different thumbprints became visible.

Barry took a piece of Scotch tape from the dispenser Ms Seal kept on the supply shelf. He pressed tape on to the graphite-coated prints. The impressions of the two prints transferred to the tape. The tape was then placed against a white card to protect the black-lined images.

"Fantastic. You're brilliant! We'll catch our villain!" Pearl was practically jumping up and down. "Wait ! Maybe the thief wore gloves."

"In May?" asked Barry, giving Pearl an exasperated look.

The next day the bell rang just as Barry entered the classroom. As soon as Pearl spotted him she motioned to him, but he put his finger to his lips, then mouthed silently, "Later."

"Ms Seal, I've chosen my science project." Barry stood at the teacher's desk. "But I need the co-operation of the whole class. I'm interested in fingerprints and how they're analysed. What I'd like to do is to collect the thumbprint of each person in the room."

Ms Seal was fingerprinted along with each class member. Using an inkpad, Barry collected the thumbprint from the hand that each person used the most.

Pearl wrote all the information on the cards Barry brought to school:

THUMB PRINT IMPRESSION

Name *Bobby Smith*

Radial Loop
Ulna Loop   RIGHT THUMB
Plain Whorl
Central Pocket Whorl
Accidental Whorl
Double Loop
Plain Arch   LEFT THUMB
Tented Arch

She was so helpful that she almost drove Barry crazy. She kept nudging him when she thought no one was looking. A few times she winked. Barry groaned. He knew all the other kids were noticing. When Bill Elevitch said with a fiendish smile, "Well, Barry, Pearl sure has a crush on you," he knew he was in for some verbal ribbing along with Pearl's more physical jabs.

At the end of the period, as the last students left the room, Pearl bubbled, "What do we do *now*?" Barry just about died as a couple of kids glanced back over their shoulders and threw him a knowing smile.

After school, Pearl and Barry stayed in the classroom, comparing the print cards with the two on the Scotch tape. One print seemed to match Pearl's own card. "Darn," she said. But when they examined the other Scotch-tape print with a magnifying glass, it didn't appear to have a duplicate on any of the THUMBPRINT IMPRESSION cards.

Barry and Pearl were stumped. "What now?" she asked.

"My dad works with computers. He's been helping the police department set up a special fingerprint program. Let's go talk to him."

Pearl and Barry arrived at Two-Bit Computer Services fifteen minutes later. Pearl explained the problem to Mr Bytes.

Barry's father compared the cards with the mystery Scotch tape print. "I agree with you two," he said finally. "You don't *seem* to have a match. But our eyes may be deceiving us. Hmmm." He patted a floppy disk. "The police have this sophisticated program that won't run on my microcomputer. Let's rework it a bit so it will. Still won't run on Nibble, I bet, though."

54

After a few minutes of typing, an image appeared on the monitor:

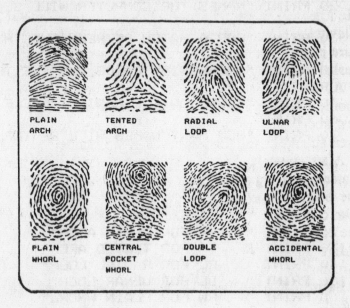

"Now," said Mr. Bytes, "you have to decide which category each student's prints fall into. The police department's computer is able to look at cards and 'read' this information."

As Barry and Pearl categorized their classmate's prints, Mr Bytes simplified the police department's program:*

---

* See debugging section for changes necessary to run this program on certain microcomputers.

```
1000 REM FINGERPRINT PROGRAM
1010 PRINT "THIS PROGRAM WILL SET UP A
FILE OF"
1020 PRINT "NAMES.THE COMPUTER WILL SEA
RCH"
1030 PRINT "FOR A MATCH BETWEEN THE THU
MBPRINT"
1040 PRINT "IMPRESSION CARDS,AND THE TH
UMBPRINT"
1050 PRINT "FOUND ON THE CABINET SHELF."
1060 PRINT
1070 PRINT "HOW MANY NAMES WILL BE INPU
T"
1080 INPUT N
1090 DIM A$(N)
1100 DIM B$(N)
1110 PRINT
1120 PRINT "   PA FOR PLAIN ARCH"
1130 PRINT "   TA FOR TENTED ARCH"
1140 PRINT "   RL FOR RADIAL LOOP"
1150 PRINT "   UL FOR ULNAR LOOP"
1160 PRINT "   PW FOR PLAIN WHORL"
1170 PRINT "   CP FOR CENTRAL POCKET WH
ORL"
1180 PRINT "   DL FOR DOUBLE LOOP"
1190 PRINT "   AW FOR ACCIDENTAL WHORL"
1200 FOR I=1 TO N
1210 PRINT "ENTER NAME"
1220 INPUT A$(I)
1230 PRINT "ENTER THUMBPRINT TYPE"
1240 INPUT B$(I)
1250 NEXT I
1260 PRINT "ENTER MYSTERY THUMBPRINT"
1270 INPUT C$
```

```
 1280 LET F=0
 1290 FOR I=1 TO N
 1300 IF B$(I)=C$ THEN GOTO 1320
 1310 GOTO 1340
 1320 PRINT " ";A$(I);" HAS THE SAME THU
MBPRINT!!!!"
 1330 LET F=1
 1340 NEXT I
 1350 IF F=1 THEN GOTO 1370
 1360 PRINT "NO THUMBPRINTS MATCH."
 1370 PRINT "SEARCH COMPLETED."
```

"Barry, why don't you debug it?" suggested his father as he answered the phone.

1060 PRINT
The word PRINT causes the computer to skip a line.

1070 PRINT "HOW MANY NAMES WILL BE INPUT"
1080 INPUT N
Barry planned to input sixteen names, so N will equal 16 in the run.

1090 DIM A$(N)
The DIM command saves spaces in memory for the sixteen names Barry will input. Those sixteen words are called strings. $ means string.

1100 DIM B$(N)
1100 sets aside spaces for each person's thumbprint type.

NOTE: Some computers need to know the number of letters in the longest string. If the longest name has 10 letters, 1090 would read:

DIM A$ (N,10)

1100 would read:

DIM B$(N,2)

as each thumbprint type has two letters.

1120 PRINT" PA FOR PLAIN ARCH"
1130 PRINT" TA FOR TENTED ARCH"
1140 PRINT" RL FOR RADIAL LOOP"
1150 PRINT" UL FOR ULNAR LOOP"
1160 PRINT" PW FOR PLAIN WHORL"
1170 PRINT" CP FOR CENTRAL POCKET WHORL"
1180 PRINT" DL FOR DOUBLE LOOP"
1190 PRINT" AW FOR ACCIDENTAL WHORL"

Here are the fingerprint-pattern interpretations. Notice the initials that stand for each type [PA, TA, etc.].

1200 FOR I=1 TO N

This FOR . . . NEXT command sets up a loop; the lines between 1200 and the end of the loop at 1250 will run N [or 16; see line 1080] times, so each student's name and type can be entered.

1220 INPUT A$(I)
1240 INPUT B$(I)

In the run A$(I) will become a name, and B$(I) will be a fingerprint type. A$ and B$ are called strings. [Some computers store their strings all in one line. This is called string emulation].

NOTE: If your computer uses string emulation, read your user's guide so you can substitute some steps in this program.

Some computers stop when the screen is full, and need an extra program line: 1245 CLS to clear the screen after each thumbprint has been entered.

1250 NEXT I
The end of a FOR . . . NEXT loop which began at 1200.

1260 PRINT "ENTER MYSTERY THUMBPRINT"
1270 INPUT C$
This is where Barry will enter the letters [RL,UL, etc.] that indicate the mystery fingerprint-type.

1280 LET F=0
This "flag" tells when a match between a student's prints and the mystery print is made. F equals 1 when the identification is positive [see 1300 to 1330].

1290 FOR I=1 TO N
1300 IF B$(I)=C$ THEN GOTO 1320
1310 GOTO 1340
1320 PRINT " "; A$(I); "HAS THE SAME THUMBPRINT!!"
1330 LET F=1
1340 NEXT I
These commands tell the computer to search for a match. Line 1320 is printed each time a match is found. Some computers do not require the GOTO command in line 1300; programmers often find it helpful to themselves to include it.

1350 IF F=1 THEN GOTO 1370
When the search is completed and there is a match, Mr Bytes' computer will skip to line 1370. Again, the program will not be affected if the GOTO is omitted in this line.

1360 PRINT "NO THUMBPRINTS MATCH"
If there is no match, the computer will print this line.

"It looks good," said Barry to Pearl, who nodded.
"Run it!" she said.

```
THIS PROGRAM WILL SET UP A FILE OF
NAMES. THE COMPUTER WILL SEARCH
FOR A MATCH BETWEEN THE THUMBPRINT
IMPRESSION CARDS,AND THE THUMBPRINT
FOUND ON THE CABINET SHELF.

HOW MANY NAMES WILL BE INPUT
?16

    PA FOR PLAIN ARCH
    TA FOR TENTED ARCH
    RL FOR RADIAL LOOP
    UL FOR ULNAR LOOP
    PW FOR PLAIN WHORL
    CP FOR CENTRAL POCKET WHORL
    DL FOR DOUBLE LOOP
    AW FOR ACCIDENTAL WHORL
ENTER NAME
?NEIL
ENTER THUMBPRINT TYPE
?RL
```

```
ENTER NAME
?TIM
ENTER THUMBPRINT TYPE
?UL
ENTER NAME
?BELINDA
ENTER THUMBPRINT TYPE
?PA
ENTER NAME
?JON
ENTER THUMBPRINT TYPE
?CP
```

Pearl, impatiently hovering over Barry as he carefully typed in the first four names and classifications, suddenly ordered, "Move over." She, who had never touched a computer before in her life, was working through the program like a pro. At a rapid rate she input the next twelve names and classifications.

"Holy macro, an instant hacker!" said Barry as she typed in the mystery print data:

```
ENTER MYSTERY THUMBPRINT
?AW
```

A second later the computer typed:

```
NO THUMBPRINTS MATCH.
SEARCH COMPLETED.
```

"Our eyes weren't wrong after all," said Mr Bytes. "None of the thumbs match the mystery one you lifted from the shelf."

Suddenly Pearl had a look that was missing only a lit-up bulb hanging over her head. "You Bytes are pretty clever with computers," she declared smugly. "But sometimes what's needed is good old-fashioned human thinking." She opened up her book bag and pulled out a miniature can of baby powder. Barry looked at her quizzically. Pearl, turning pink, said, "My feet get itchy at school."

She picked up Barry's right hand. Oh no, he thought, what's with this crazy girl? She pressed Barry's thumb againt the black desk top. Then she sprinkled powder on the print. Off came the goose pin with its real feather tail.

"Wow," said Pearl.

"Holy macro," said Barry.

"You're a clear-thinking young lady," said Mr Bytes. "Barry, in the future keep your own big paws off an area you're lifting prints from!" Barry's print was a perfect match with the mystery print lifted from the glass shelf.

"I think we've narrowed the situation down," said Pearl. "We now have a criminal who doesn't have fingers."

Barry wished Pearl wouldn't be so dramatic. Then he sat up. "Wait a minute. Let me think." They waited while Barry thought. He could picture himself in the classroom, seated next to Belinda as she dried her fingernails. Then he remembered June and Belinda washing their hands. He could visualize Neil leaving the back room with a couple of sheets of graph paper in his hand.

"Uh-oh," said Mr Bytes.

"What's wrong?" asked Pearl.

"Wrong? Nothing," answered Mr Bytes. "When Barry looks like a cat that just swallowed the canary, he's solved a mystery."

DO YOU KNOW
what Barry remembered?

Barry recalled that Belinda didn't help Pearl with the shelf when it slipped off its supports because she had just polished her nails. Yet Belinda was sitting with her palms *up*, a rather unusual way to dry nails. He decided that she'd coated her fingertips with the colourless nail polish so her prints couldn't condemn her when the theft was noticed.

She entered the back room, left a smudge or two that Barry thought Pearl made when cleaning the shelf, and took the bag.

When confronted, Belinda apologized and returned Pearl's cell. Pearl asked her why she did it. Belinda explained that she hoped to be a scientist some day, but had never even been in a research laboratory. The contest gave her that opportunity.

Belinda felt terrible about what she'd done. Pearl, who had been ready to sentence the criminal to fifty years, quickly forgave her classmate, and when Ms Seal gave Belinda a week's detention, Pearl suggested to the teacher that Belinda instead carry Pearl's books for seven days. Belinda was grateful.

Barry's mother, when she heard the story, offered Belinda an after-school job in her lab, washing glassware. Belinda was thrilled.

Belinda finally turned in a project of her own —

about the workings of the sweat glands right below the fingertips which make an "ink" that leaves fingerprints.

Pearl's beautifully constructed cell won the competition.

4.

Missing Books

"Mark," Dr Bytes said to her husband as she passed him the succotash, "I really should run over to the lab to see if that new sea urchin experiment is working properly." The Bytes were having dinner.

"Mom, could you drop me off at the library on the way?" asked Barry as he swallowed a hunk of tomato. "I've got to get to work on my project." He had to do a report on decomposition.

"Take smaller bites, Barry," said Mr Bytes as he turned to his wife. "Jill, you two go on as soon as you're done eating. Brent and I'll take care of the dishes."

Brent, astonished at his father's offer, quickly pushed back his chair, knocking it over: "Say, maybe I'd better go with Mom," he said as he picked up the chair. "I've got to do my science book review you know. It's due next Thursday."

Mr Bytes laughed. "All right, Brent. Just make sure you come home with a book under your arm. Otherwise I might think you're just trying to get out of scrubbing the broiler pan."

"Dad, how can you *say* such a thing!" retorted Brent indignantly.

At the library, Brent began looking through magazines as Barry sat down in front of the library's

terminal. The computer could tell him what books the library had on the subject of decomposition, and where in the library they were located. The readout also would indicate if they were checked out.

Barry started typing on the keyboard. He chose six books from the readout, then asked the computer if they were available.

All six books were checked out. Holy macro, he thought. Everyone in the school must be working on decomposition. I didn't know there was so much interest in rot. Pretty rotten for me. He chuckled.

"Are you finding what you want, Barry dear?" Mrs Bumble, the librarian who drove all the kids crazy, stood behind him and peered in her nearsighted way at the monitor.

Barry hated it when people read over his shoulder. "No, I'm not," he said. "Every single book I need is checked out. I can't believe it. All six of them, so far. But I'll keep trying."

This time he checked for books under COMPOST. The computer's readout showed that of the seven books on compost, two were available. He asked for a printout, tore it off, and headed for the bookshelves.

Mrs Bumble was having some trouble with the computer as Barry returned to check out his two books. "Just a minute, dear," she said. "I've got to input my user's number and password so the computer'll know it's me calling."

Barry mentally rolled his eyes towards heaven. Mrs Bumble and a computer were an unusual combination. He smiled politely as she explained that the library's terminal was connected by cables with a huge computer system in Ellenville, an hour's drive away.

At that moment other libraries and schools also hooked into Ellenville were using the main computer. That meant that Mrs Bumble—and Barry—had to wait their turn.

Finally she entered the data, then handed the books back to him.

Barry had plopped into an easy chair and was turning pages in *The Whole Compost Guide* as Brent walked up: "Are you ready to go? I am. It seems like every book I want is checked out."

"Me too." Barry looked around at the tall bookshelves. "It sure looks as if there are a lot of books here. But the computer doesn't agree." He stood up. "Let's go home."

The boys passed Mrs Bumble's checkout desk on their way to the exit. Garth Dingleheimer stood there, with a forlorn look behind his eyeglasses and about ten books piled in front of him. "I'm sorry, Garth." The librarian shook her white curls. "But enough is enough! I can't let you check out any more books until you've brought back all your overdue ones. You've got so many out that you'll have to ask your mother to drive you over with them." The Bytes managed to slip out before the Bumble began a friendly, but for sure lengthy, conversation with them.

After school the next day, Barry spotted Brent walking ahead of him towards the library. "Trying again, huh?" Barry asked his brother as he caught up. "Me too."

As they turned the corner, they saw Garth, his eyeglasses askew, with books scattered on the ground around him. "Holy macro, Garth. *You* sure found what you needed," said Barry. Brent—sympathetic

72

with anyone who dropped, spilled or tripped over things like he constantly did—helped Garth pick up the books. The boy straightened his glasses and hurried off.

I hope I'm as lucky, thought Barry as they entered the library's main reading room.

"Mr Darwin, I'm having trouble with my report." Cathy smiled at her science teacher. Cathy always smiled. "I can't seem to find the information I need."

"Cathy, how can that be? With the town's new library computer system you don't even have to search for appropriate books. You're given a listing of them, for goodness sake."

Cathy's smile broke through again. "Unfortunately, only two of the books listed under the CALCIUM heading are available. The rest are checked out. And those two aren't so great."

"Ye gods and little fishes!" Mr Darwin burst forth. "There must be twenty books on that list. I can't imagine that everybody in Lamont Landing chose to learn about calcium this week." He thought for a minute. "It sounds as if some class is studying calcium. I'll check with the other teachers at lunch."

"You'd better ask them about garbage too," said Barry. Mr Darwin looked at him like he was off his rocker. "I went to the library two days in a row and only found a couple of books under COMPOST. Someone's really interested in smelly stuff. Aside from myself, that is."

"And Nansen, Mr Darwin," Philip, a shy boy, said softly.

"Nansen?" asked the teacher.

73

"Remember, I'm doing my report on Fridtjof Nansen, the famous Norwegian scientist?"

"You mean to tell me that there are no books to do with Nansen?"

"There are encyclopedias. But the computer says the library has five different books to do with Nansen. All were checked out, except one."

"Strange . . ," said Mr Darwin. "Now, class, please open your books at page fifty-two . . . ."

Brent and Barry were playing gin rummy in the living room as their mother walked in the back door. "Hi boys, I'm home." Dr Bytes dropped her notebooks on the kitchen desk, opened the fridge and poured herself a tall glass of lemonade.

"Hi, Mom. How was your day with the sea urchins?" Barry got himself some lemonade too.

"Thorny." Dr Bytes was shuffling through the mail. "Barry, you've got one, two, three . . . seven!—overdue-book postcards from the library. How about gathering the books together right now and putting them in your backpack. You can drop them off on your way home from school tomorrow."

"What?" Barry looked surprised. "What books do I have checked out?" He took the cards from his mother. "This is crazy. I've never *heard* of any of these books."

"What books?" Brent headed for the fridge. On the way he grabbed a handful of chocolate chip cookies, dropped one on the floor, and wolfed down the rest.

"They must be ones you checked out, Brent. I don't know anything about them." Barry handed his brother the computer-printed postcards.

"They're not mine," said Brent, accidentally stepping on the cookie. "I returned all the books I checked out."

Barry, generally pretty even-tempered, was getting a little hot under the collar. "First I can't find any of the books I need, and now I'm supposed to have books I don't even want. I'm going to the library right now to straighten this out." He shoved the postcards into his pocket and headed for the door.

When he got inside the library, Cecil, a red-headed boy who was in Barry's gym class, stood talking to the librarian: "Mrs Bumble, I've received a pile of overdue notices for books I've never heard of."

"Cecil, that's impossible. You know we're on a computerized system now. It's out of human hands. If the computer says you checked out these books, then you did."

Brother! thought Barry. This doesn't sound too great. While he waited for Cecil and Mrs Bumble to stop arguing, his eyes wandered around the library and ended on Mrs Bumble's bulletin board, where she had computer instruction sheets and the library's user number. Cecil was still talking. Barry, recognizing a lost cause, left without even speaking to the librarian.

On his way home, he thought about what Mrs Bumble had said. She was right about computers, but she forgot that they can only respond to human input.

Barry went to his room to think. On his dresser was the computer printout he got at the library the day before. He noticed that all the books that were checked out had borrower's identification numbers next to them. Then he glanced at his library card, number 5069. He looked at the printout again. One of the books he particularly wanted to read for his report, *Lots of Rot*, was checked out—to him! What's goin' on here? he wondered.

The next day was Saturday. Barry was at the library before Mrs Bumble. He waited as she unlocked the door, and they went in together.

Mrs Bumble and Barry had a long talk that exhausted even Mrs Bumble. Once the librarian pointed to an index card tacked to the bulletin board behind her desk. Barry nodded his head. She placed the card in her desk drawer.

Several times during the discussion, Barry walked over to the computer terminal with Mrs Bumble and typed. Mrs Bumble began shaking her head, and ended nodding rapidly. Then the librarian typed. Both read the readout.

Mrs Bumble and Barry smiled at one another. Then they shook hands.

Barry and Mrs Bumble had solved the mystery of the missing books! HAVE YOU?

Someone was checking out books and not returning them. Yet false information was fed into the computer that the books *had* been returned. To explain the books' absence from the shelves, the culprit fed data into the computer which indicated that other people had then checked out the books. This is why Barry received overdue notices for books he'd never heard of.

Barry realized that the library computer's security had been "compromised"—someone other than Mrs Bumble had figured out how to add and subtract information, using the library's user number plus a password.

Both the school's and the library's computer terminals were hooked into the same large central mainframe computer in Ellenville, thirty miles away. This meant that a student, using a school terminal, could change library data, if he had the correct number and password.

Once Barry realized what was going on, he remembered that Mrs Bumble had told Garth Dingleheimer that he could not check out any books until his mound of overdue books was returned. Yet the very next day after school Barry saw Garth coming out of the library with about ten books; Brent had helped him pick them up when they fell.

This suggested to Barry that Garth may have fiddled with the library's data. So Barry and Mrs Bumble checked with the computer. Sure enough, each book that was supposedly checked out to Barry had previously been checked out to Garth.

But why would Garth, a nice guy, do such a thing?

Garth loved to read. He constantly checked out piles of books and hated to return them. Even at three cents a day, his fines were huge, and he didn't have enough money to pay them. With computerized overdue notices stuck in his wallet and hidden in his top drawer in between his underwear, Garth had no idea what to do.

When he noticed Mrs Bumble's user number on the bulletin board, he decided to try to alter the record to show he had returned his books, and that others had checked them out later. His solution made him unhappy but he was desperate.

All he needed was the library's three-letter password.

He worked on that during lunchtime on the school computer.

Garth, a bit of a hacker, knew that most computers use a code called ASCII, pronounced *ask-ee: American Standard Code for Information Interchange*. In ASCII, a two-digit number stands for each symbol and letter.

This is the ASCII code:

```
        HORIZONTAL KEY
        0   1   2   3   4   5   6   7   8   9
   30               !   "   `   $   %   &   '
   40   (   )   *   +   ,   _   .   /   0   1
   50   2   3   4   5   6   7   8   9   :   ;
   60   <   =   >   ?   @   A   B   C   D   E
   70   F   G   H   I   J   K   L   M   N   O
   80   P   Q   R   S   T   U   V   W   X   Y
   90   Z
```

VERTICAL KEY

Read the chart both across and down, and add the numbers together. For example, B would be 66 [60 from the vertical key, plus 6 from the horizontal key] Q is 81. A comma [,] would be written 44.

Garth planned to discover the library's password using ASCII. He wrote his program:

```
1000 FOR I=1 TO 26
1010 FOR J=1 TO 26
1020 FOR K=1 TO 26
1030 PRINT CHR$(64+I);
1040 PRINT CHR$(64+J);
1050 PRINT CHR$(64+K);
1060 PRINT " ";
1070 NEXT K
1080 NEXT J
1090 NEXT I
```

The debug was pretty simple:

```
1000 FOR I = 1 TO 26
1010 FOR J = 1 TO 26
1020 FOR K = 1 TO 26
```

FOR . . . NEXT statements will begin a loop, in this case three loops, "nesting" one within another. This is how each letter of the alphabet will be tried out as the 1st, 2nd, and 3rd letter of Mrs Bumble's unknown code word.

```
1030 PRINT CHR$(64+I);
1040 PRINT CHR$(64+J);
1050 PRINT CHR$(64+K);
```

This tells the computer to print ASCII code numbers starting with 65 [64 plus another number] because A = 65 in ASCII.

```
1060 PRINT " ";
```

Space is needed between each possible three-letter word in the run.

```
1070 NEXT K
1080 NEXT J
1090 NEXT I
```

1070,1080 and 1090 check the FOR . . . NEXT loop to see if it is okay to continue.

NOTE: This program will work on most micro-computers. A few, however, do not use ASCII code.

The computer typed the run in a matter of seconds.

```
AAA AAB AAC AAD AAE AAF AAG AAH AAI AAJ
AAK AAL AAM AAN AAO AAP AAQ AAR AAS AAT
AAU AAV AAW AAX AAY AAZ ABA ABB ABC ABD
ABE ABF ABG ABH ABI ABJ ABK ABL ABM ABN
ABO ABP ABQ ABR ABS ABT ABU ABV ABW ABX
ABY ABZ ACA ACB ACC ACD ACE ACF ACG ACH
ACI ACJ ACK ACL ACM ACN ACO ACP ACQ ACR
ACS ACT ACU ACV ACW ACX ACY ACZ ADA ADB
ADC ADD ADE ADF ADG ADH ADI ADJ ADK ADL
ADM ADN ADO ADP ADQ ADR ADS ADT ADU ADV
ADW ADX ADY ADZ AEA AEB AEC AED AEE AEF
AEG AEH AEI AEJ AEK AEL AEM AEN AEO AEP
AEQ AER AES AET AEU AEV AEW AEX AEY AEZ
AFA AFB AFC AFD AFE AFF AFG AFH AFI AFJ
AFK AFL AFM AFN AFO AFP AFQ AFR AFS AFT
AFU AFV AFW AFX AFY AFZ AGA AGB AGC AGD
AGE AGF AGG AGH AGI AGJ AGK AGL A··      ··R
AGO AGP AGQ AGR AGS AGT AGU A·        ···R
AGY AGZ AHA AHB AHC AHD A·        ··XA AXB
AHI AHJ AHK AHL AHM A·           ·XJ AXK AXL
AHS AHT AHU AHV ·        ·   AXS AXT AXU AXV
AIC AID AIF        ·  AYB AYC AYD AYE AYF
AIM AIN        ·J AYK AYL AYM AYN AYO AYP
AI·       ··S AYT AYU AYV AYW AYX AYY AYZ
      ·ZB AZC AZD AZE AZF AZG AZH AZI AZJ
·ZK AZL AZM AZN AZO AZP AZQ AZR AZS AZT
AZU AZV AZW AZX AZY AZZ BAA BAB BAC BAD
BAE BAF BAG BAH BAI BAJ BAK BAL BAM BAN
BAO BAP BAQ BAR BAS BAT BAU BAV BAW BAX
BAY BAZ BBA BBB BBC BBD BBE BBF BBG BBH
BBI BBJ BBK BBL BBM BBN BBO BBP BBQ BBR
BBS BBT BBU BBV BBW BBX BBY BBZ BCA BCB
BCC BCD BCE BCF BCG BCH BCI BCJ BCK BCL
BCM BCN BCO BCP BCQ BCR BCS BCT BCU BCV
BCW BCX BCY BCZ BDA BDB BDC BDD BDE BDF
BDG BDH BDI BDJ BDK BDL BDM BDN BDO BDP
```

When the printout reached the word BEE, Ellenville's mainframe computer responded. Garth input Mrs Bumble's user number, and was able to change the library's records.

Garth was almost happy when his devious deeds were exposed. He had felt so guilty. He began working in the library after school in order to pay his fines. He also smiled patiently as the librarian lectured to him for what seemed like ten hours (but was really only ten minutes) on America's free library system and how children in other countries have to pay rental fees to borrow books.

Mrs Bumble got a new user number and kept it tucked away. She changed her password every week.

Barry dressed himself as a compost pile when he presented his rot report to the class. He got an A but everyone refused to sit next to him at lunchtime.

5.

A Fishy Business

School holidays had just begun. Brent Bytes was lounging in bed considering not getting up all summer when his mother peeked through the crack in the door.

"Brent, are you awake? Elana's downstairs and is dying to talk to you."

Brent sighed, crawled out of bed, and struggled into a T-shirt and blue jeans. He stumbled down the first ten steps, then tripped and manoeuvered the final three in a sitting position. Before he could say a word, Elana burst out, "Brent, I'm so excited! I've got a summer job. Whoopee!"

Brent awoke quickly. "Where?"

"At A Fishy Business."

Brent knew that that was the name of the new aquarium shop a couple of doors down from Two-Bit Computer Services.

"Hey, that's great, Elana."

Elana was dying to work this summer, so she could put more money into her savings account.

"You haven't heard the best part. You've got a job there too."

"Me?" Brent couldn't believe his ears.

Elana nodded. "What we'll mainly be doing is hauling sea water from the bay for the aquariums. Mrs Alewife, the lady who owns A Fishy Business, must

have a hundred tanks. She wants to start the saltwater aquariums with water that doesn't have chlorine added to it."

"Wow! When do we start? How much is she paying us? How many hours a day do we work?"

Elana grinned. "I knew you'd be excited. Let's go. She wants us there in a half an hour. I'll tell you all about it on the way."

When they reached A Fishy Business, Mrs Alewife had a wagon and six large buckets with lids waiting for them. Brent took the handle and he and Elana headed for the bay.

On the way they passed the beach. It was low tide and kids were building dribble castles in the newly exposed sand. Brent said, "This job is really terrific. We'll earn good money and still have afternoons free to go swimming."

As they collected water around the point from where the children were playing, the noon whistle sounded. Brent said, "Why don't we celebrate and buy ourselves lunch at the Fishmonger's Café? I could use a big juicy clam roll."

The two friends took the covered buckets of salt water back to A Fishy Business and carefully poured them into two tanks the way Mrs Alewife told them to. Amazingly, Brent didn't spill a drop. Then they checked the water's temperature and added queen angelfish to one tank and neon gobi fish to the other.

By one o'clock they were on their way to the Fishmonger's Café. They both agreed that their summer vacation was starting out beautifully.

But when they reported to work the next day, a glance at the angelfish and neonfish tanks caused their sweet frames of mind to turn sour. All the fish were floating with their bellies facing the ceiling. "Uh-oh," said Elana as she saw Mrs Alewife coming towards them from the back of the store.

A quick discussion between the store owner and her two young employees did not throw any light on the reason for the tragedy. Brent and Elana collected the water in the bay around the point from the swimming beach, just as Mrs Alewife told them to. They poured the water into the tanks, then carefully put in the fish after checking the water temperatures.

Mrs Alewife said, "I certainly don't blame you two. You did exactly as you were told. But you can understand that I don't want you to collect any more water for me until we figure out what happened. I can't afford to send my angels to heaven and have the lights go out on my neons." Brent and Elana barely cracked a smile at Mrs Alewife's attempt to cheer them up. They took their one day's pay with them as they left, feeling miserable.

Instead of going home, they headed straight for Dr Bytes' laboratory. If anyone would know what caused the fish to die, it would be Brent's marine-biologist mother.

"I have no idea," said Dr Bytes after Brent explained. "There's a new discharge pipe from our labs to that bay area, away from the beach. But the seawater is tested regularly and it's fine." Brent nodded. He remembered seeing scientists collecting water in the bay from time to time, from a rowing boat. Dr Bytes, seeing the disappointment on his face, said, "Let me think it over and we'll talk about it when I come home."

"Well, listen," said Elana to Brent as they walked past the boat yard. "Let's get our suits on and go down to the beach. I read in the paper that yesterday's low tide was the lowest we'll have all year. That means that today'll be great for building a giant dribble castle." She added, "No sense wasting the day worrying about something we can't do anything about."

"No thanks. I plan to brood." Brent stared at the pavement all the way to his house. As soon as he got home, he went upstairs to his room and sprawled out on his bed, where he did his best thinking. Somehow water from the lab's drainage pipe was responsible for the dead fish, he felt sure. But the bay water was carefully tested. Then he remembered something, or rather, a couple of things.

Brent ran downstairs, called his mother, and asked if she could find out how frequently the lab released its used water. Dr Bytes already knew. The pump was turned on every day at noon to discharge waste liquids and old seawater from the experiment tanks filled with marine specimens. Then Brent asked her to find out the dates that the bay water had been tested. He held on while she checked.

Armed with this information, he climbed the staircase, sat down in front of Nibble, and began to type. In a half hour he had a program: *(See over)*

```
1000 PRINT "THIS PROGRAM SHOWS THE HIGH
EST AND"
1010 PRINT "LOWEST TIDES OF EACH MONTH.
THE"
1020 PRINT "DATES SCIENTISTS TESTED WAT
ER,AND THE"
1030 PRINT "DAY WATER WAS COLLECTED FOR
A FISHY"
1040 PRINT "BUSINESS IS PLOTTED."
1050 FOR I=1 TO 2000
1060 NEXT I
1070 FOR I=1 TO 32
1080 PRINT
1090 NEXT I
1100 DIM A(31,11)
1110 FOR I=1 TO 31
1120 FOR J=1 TO 11
1130 LET A(I,J)=0
1140 NEXT J
1150 NEXT I
1160 LET H=1
1170 LET T=1
1180 FOR D=1 TO 31
1190 LET X=1
1200 IF D=1 THEN 1230
1210 IF D=17 THEN 1230
1220 GOTO 1250
1230 LET X=2
1240 GOTO 1280
1250 IF D=25 THEN 1270
1260 GOTO 1280
1270 LET X=3
1280 IF H<=1 THEN 1300
1290 GOTO 1330
1300 LET H=1
1310 LET T=1
1320 GOTO 1370
1330 IF H>=11 THEN 1350
```

```
1340 GOTO 1370
1350 LET H=11
1360 LET T=-3
1370 LET A(D,H)=X
1380 LET H=H+T
1390 NEXT D
1400 PRINT "(HIGHEST TIDE)"
1410 FOR J=1 TO 11
1420 FOR I=1 TO 31
1430 LET X=A(I,J)
1440 IF X=0 THEN 1460
1450 GOTO 1480
1460 PRINT " ";
1470 GOTO 1570
1480 IF X=1 THEN 1500
1490 GOTO 1520
1500 PRINT ".";
1510 GOTO 1570
1520 IF X=2 THEN 1540
1530 GOTO 1560
1540 PRINT "S";
1550 GOTO 1570
1560 PRINT "K";
1570 NEXT I
1580 PRINT
1590 NEXT J
1600 PRINT "(LOWEST TIDE)"
1610 PRINT "          11111222223          1111122
2223"
1620 PRINT "13579135791357912468024680 2
4680"
1630 PRINT "              MAY              JU
NE"
1640 PRINT "S=WHEN THE SCIENTISTS TESTE
D WATER."
1650 PRINT "K=WHEN THE KIDS COLLECTED W
ATER."
1660 END
```

Then he debugged it:

```
1050 FOR I=1 TO 2000
1060 NEXT I
```
This FOR . . . NEXT loop makes the computer wait a few seconds, so Brent can read the words. If you have a very fast computer, you may need to increase the number 2000.

```
1070 FOR I=1 TO 32
1080 PRINT
1090 NEXT I
```
Nibble needs the "garbage" totally removed from the screen before creating a graph. When line 1080 is typed in, the print on the screen should roll up. This loop will clear 32 lines of space.
NOTE: If this doesn't "scroll" the words off the screen, replace these three lines with the single line: 1070 CLS

```
1100 DIM A(31,11)
```
The DIM or dimension command sets up an array, or a table of numbers.

```
1110 FOR I=1 TO 31
1120 FOR J=1 TO 11
1130 LET A(I,J)=0
1140 NEXT J
1150 NEXT I
```
These FOR . . . NEXT lines will set the numbers in the array to zero, making the graph empty.

```
1160 LET H=1
```
H is the height of the tide on any one day.

1170 LET T=1
T will help determine how to plot the rise and fall of the tide on the graph.

1180 FOR D=1 TO 31
1190 LET X=1
1200 IF D=1 THEN 1230
1210 IF D=17 THEN 1230
1220 GOTO 1250
1230 LET X=2
1240 GOTO 1280
1250 IF D=25 THEN 1270
1260 GOTO 1280
1270 LET X=3
1280 IF H<=1 THEN 1300
1290 GOTO 1330
1300 LET H=1
1310 LET T=1
1320 GOTO 1370
1330 IF H>=11 THEN 1350
1340 GOTO 1370
1350 LET H=11
1360 LET T=−3
1370 LET A(D,H)=X
1380 LET H=H + T
1390 NEXT D

The FOR . . . NEXT loop begins at 1180. It will help plot the days water was collected by Brent and Elana [3], and by the scientists [2], and days when nothing happened [1]. The loop ends at 1390. 1200 IF D = 1 THEN 1230 tells the computer to skip to line 1230. Some computers need the word GOTO after THEN.

(Line 1280, 1330 and 1370 through 1390 are discussed further below).

1280 IF H<=1 THEN 1300
1330 IF H>=11 THEN 1350
These two statements [plus the lines following them] tell Nibble whether tides are rising or falling.

1370 LET A(D,H)=X
The type of day—1, 2 or 3—[see 1190, 1230, 1270] gets placed in the array here.

1380 LET H=H+ T
The height of the tide must vary. This will change it.

1390 NEXT D
The loop which began at 1180 ends here.

1400 PRINT "(HIGHEST TIDE)"
This line labels the graph.

1420 FOR I=1 TO 31
1430 LET X=A(I,J)
1440 IF X=0 THEN 1460
1450 GOTO 1480
1460 PRINT " " ;
1470 GOTO 1570
1480 IF X=1 THEN 1500
1490 GOTO 1520
1500 PRINT " ." ;
1510 GOTO 1570
1520 IF X=2 THEN 1540
1530 GOTO 1560

1540 PRINT "S";
1550 GOTO 1570
1560 PRINT "K";
1570 NEXT I
This FOR . . . NEXT loop is within the loop which started at 1410. These nested loops will print the K [for when the kids collected water], S [the days the scientists tested] or a . for all other days.

1580 PRINT
The graph will drop one line lower because of this PRINT.

1590 NEXT J
Here the J loop ends [the I loop is "nested" within this J loop] which started at 1410.

1600 PRINT "(LOWEST TIDE)"
1610 PRINT "   11111222223   11111222223"
1620 PRINT "13579135791357912468024680246808"
1630 PRINT "   MAY   JUNE"
1640 PRINT "S = WHEN THE SCIENTISTS TESTED WATER."
1650 PRINT "K = WHEN THE KIDS COLLECTED WATER."
These lines print out the labels and dates under the graph. ⅔ means 21. With May below it, it becomes May 21st. Brent had to be careful to skip the correct number of spaces on lines 1610, 1620 and 1630 or the graph would not line up.

Some computers have fewer characters to a line than Nibble. If Brent were working on one of those, the layout of the titles at the top of the graph, and the key at the bottom, would look different. [A devoted hacker like Brent would work at debugging it, of course!]

The graph, with its key, is 18 lines long. If he were using a computer with a display of fewer than 18 lines, Brent would leave out the key (lines 1640 and 1650).

Finally he ran it. Luckily we have Nibble, he said to himself as he typed RUN. Computers with less than 32 characters per line can't handle this program.

```
THIS PROGRAM SHOWS THE HIGHEST AND
LOWEST TIDES OF EACH MONTH.THE
DATES SCIENTISTS TESTED WATER,AND THE
DAY WATER WAS COLLECTED FOR A FISHY
BUSINESS IS PLOTTED.
(HIGHEST TIDE)
S               .                    .
     .               .    .      . .  .
        .              S              .
        .                 .
     .         .               .
        .       .                  .
        .        .               .
           .       .             .
              .                 .
                .             .
                            .
                .                   .
              .                 K
(LOWEST TIDE)
        11111222223     11111222223
1357913579135791246802468024680
          MAY              JUNE
S=WHEN THE SCIENTISTS TESTED WATER.
K=WHEN THE KIDS COLLECTED WATER.
```

"I see what happened!" said Brent. DO YOU?

Brent realized that he and Elana had collected the water for A Fishy Business during an extremely low tide. (Remember, Elana had read in the paper that the lowest tide of the year was on the day they collected water.) The children heard the noon whistle as they reached the bay. Just as Brent and Elana were scooping up water, the pipe was discharging.

The combination of a super-low tide and the release of water from the lab resulted in a high concentration of waste chemicals, for there was only shallow water for the chemicals to mix with.

The scientists collected water to test from a boat — where the water was deeper and the mixing in of the chemicals would be better. Also, they got their water samples during days when even the low tide was fairly high (see Brent's program).

Dr Bytes spoke to the laboratory administrator, who scheduled the release of the waste water so that it would coincide with each day's high tide.

Elana and Brent explained the solution of the mystery to Mrs Alewife, who didn't know there was a pipe in the bay. The children were rehired and collected water only at high tide, and from around the other side of the point, near the beach.

Mrs Alewife did a great deal of business that summer. Elana, the secret hacker, saved thirty dollars towards buying her own Nibble. Brent gave his parents a beautiful saltwater aquarium for their anniversary.

The Bytes Brothers
Micro-Dictionary

ARRAY
: When data is organized in a series of rows and columns, an array has been created.

ASCII
: An acronym for *AMERICAN STANDARD CODE for INFORMATION INTERCHANGE*. A computer coding system that substitutes numbers for letters.

BASIC
: The most commonly used micro-computer language is BASIC which stands for *BEGINNER'S ALL-PURPOSE SYMBOLIC INSTRUCTION CODE*. Its language includes commands like FOR . . . NEXT and GOTO.

BIT
: Stands for *BINARY DIGIT*. One of the computer's on- and off-switches that can be used to store information, play games or run a Bytes Brothers program.

BYTE

A set of eight bits—on/off switches—is called a BYTE.

CIRCUIT

A system where electricity flows in a specific pattern.

COMPUTER

A machine with a memory, made up of bytes. A COMPUTER can make decisions, and can handle both words and numbers; a calculator cannot. And, unlike a calculator, a COMPUTER can be programmed to do the same thing over and over (see LOOP).

COMPUTER SCIENCE

The science/engineering profession that involves computers.

DATA

Facts a computer processes. You feed DATA into a computer, and get information from it.

DEBUG

To identify, find and correct errors in a computer program.

DIM

DIM is a programming instruction that stands for *DIMENSION*. It sets up a table of columns and rows within the computer's memory. DIM can be used to clear all of a monitor's row-and-column spaces.

FLOPPY DISK A square, thin envelope containing a flat plastic disk which resembles a 45 rpm phonograph record. Computerdata is stored on FLOPPY DISKS.

FOR . . . NEXT This computer statement begins a loop that will repeat itself any number of times it is programmed to.

GARBAGE Unwanted, false, meaningless data.

GOTO GOTO tells the computer to move on to a certain line.

IF. . . THEN A programming statement in which IF something is true, THEN the computer gets special instructions; if it is false, the computer drops to the next line.

INPUT Information fed into a computer by humans, or by other computers. In a program INPUT causes a ? or other "prompt" to appear on the monitor during the run, and tells the computer to wait for a response. (See PROMPT.)

INT   A BASIC function that truncates a number; it removes (but does not round off) the numerals to the right of the decimal point, leaving an integer or whole number (see TRUNCATE).

LOOP   A computer action that keeps repeating itself.

MACRO   A set of instructions given to a computer. MACRO is also a computer language.

MAINFRAME   A large computer with many capabilities, used by governments, corporations, banks and hospitals. Different groups can take turns, or time-share, on the same mainframe.

MICRO   *MICRO* means small. A home computer is called a microcomputer.

MINI-COMPUTER   In between a micro and a mainframe is the mini, usually a great deal more powerful than a microcomputer.

MODEM | Stands for **MODULATOR-DEMODULATOR**. A telephone receiver is placed cradle-like in a MODEM that is connected to a computer. This allows that computer to "talk" to another computer—which might be thousands of miles away—through telephone lines. Microcomputers' MODEMS usually are a bundle of circuits within a rectangular box. Mainframe computers have built-in MODEMS.

MONITOR | A computer terminal's screen, also called a CRT, for cathode ray tube. A home computer's *MONITOR* is the T.V. screen (which has a CRT inside).

NEXT | See definition for FOR . . . NEXT.

PRINT | Whatever follows PRINT in a program and is surrounded by quotation marks will be printed.

PRINTOUT | One of the methods a computer has to communicate. A *PRINTOUT* is letters and numbers on paper. (See READOUT.)

PROGRAM   A set of logical step-by-step instructions given to a computer in language it can understand.

PROMPT   The Computer displays a ? or other PROMPT, then waits for data-input. (see INPUT.)

READOUT   This is how the computer communicates with humans; letters and numbers displayed on the monitor are called READOUT. When printed on paper it is called PRINTOUT.

REM   REM is short for *REMARK*. In the run, computers ignore REMs. When a computer program says REM, it is going to make a remark or give information rather than take an actual step in solving a problem.

RUN   This command starts a program.

STRING   A group of letters, numbers or symbols, such as BRENT or T5. In the program, string variables must begin with a letter and end with a $, like A$.

TERMINAL

A combined input and output system humans and computers use to communicate through to one another. A keyboard, monitor, disk drive and printer are together called a TERMINAL.

TRUNCATE

To cut off. The number 45.987 becomes 45 when TRUNCATED (see INT).

VARIABLE

A variable's value can change. Suppose A is a variable whose value is 4. Divide it by 2 and the variable A then equals 2.